BUD THE SPUD

The song "Bud the Spud" performed by Stompin' Tom Connors is available
from EMI Music Canada on the following albums:
Bud the Spud C4-92974
Live at the Horseshoe C4-93048
A Proud Canadian S4-80007

Nimbus Publishing Limited
PO Box 9166
Halifax, NS   B3K 5M8
(902) 455-4286

National Library of Canada Cataloguing in Publication

Connors, Stompin' Tom, 1936-
Bud the Spud / Stompin' Tom Connors ; illustrations by Brenda Jones.

Originally published: Charlottetown, P.E.I. : Ragweed Press, c1994.
ISBN 1-55109-429-0

I. Jones, Brenda, 1953- II. Title.

PS8555.O5577B84 2002   jC811'.54   C2002-902728-4   PZ7

STOMPIN' TOM CONNORS
BUD THE SPUD

ILLUSTRATIONS BY BRENDA JONES

NIMBUS
PUBLISHING

It's Bud the Spud, from the bright red mud,

Rollin' down the highway smilin',

The spuds are big on the back of Bud's rig,

They're from Prince Edward Island,

They're from Prince Edward Island.

Now from Charlottetown, or from Summerside,

They load him down for the big long ride;

He jumps in his cab and he's off with the pride—

Sebagoes;

He's gotta catch the boat to make Tormentine,

Then he hits up that old New Brunswick line,

Through Montreal he comes just a-flyin',

With another big load of potatoes.

Now the Ontario Provincial Police

Don't think much of Bud...

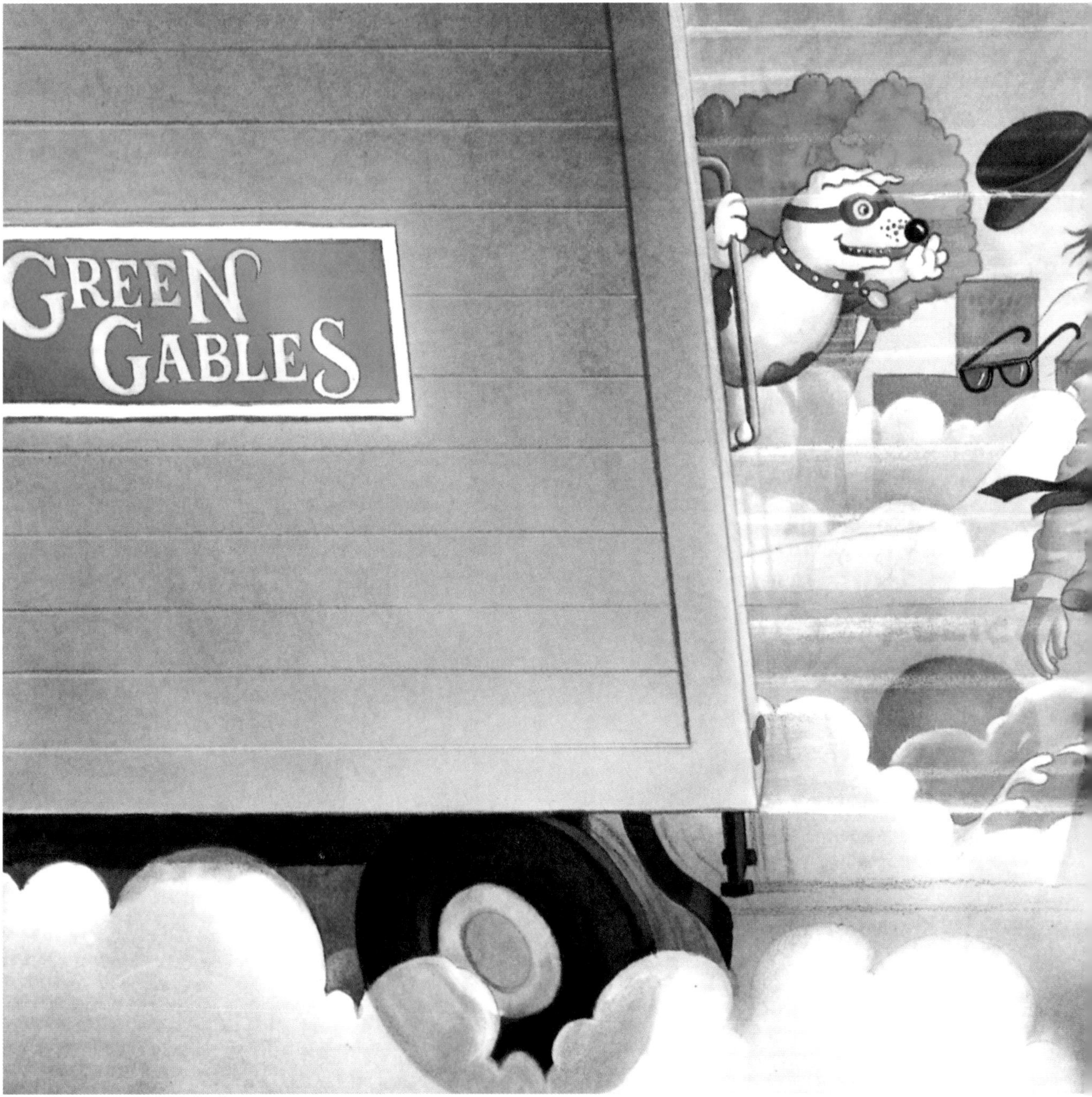
GREEN GABLES

Yeah, the cops have been lookin'

For the son of a gun

That's been rippin' the tar

Off the four-O-one;

They know the name on the truck

Shines up in the sun—"Green Gables";

But he hits Toronto and it's seven o'clock,

When he backs 'er up again

At the terminal dock,

And the boys gather 'round

Just to hear him talk

About another big load of potatoes.

Now I know a lot of people from east to west

That like the spuds from the Island best,

'Cause they'll stand up to the hardest test—

Right on the table;

So when you see that big truck a-rollin' by,

Wave your hand or kinda wink your eye,

'Cause that's Bud the Spud, from old P.E.I.,

With another big load of potatoes.

It's Bud the Spud, from the bright red mud,

Rollin' down the highway smilin',

Because he's got another big load

Of the best doggone potatoes

That's ever been growed,

And they're from Prince Edward Island,

They're from Prince Edward Island.

BUD
THE
SPUD

It's Bud the Spud, from the bright red mud,
Rollin' down the highway smilin',
The spuds are big on the back of Bud's rig,
They're from Prince Edward Island,
They're from Prince Edward Island.

Now from Charlottetown, or from Summerside,
They load him down for the big long ride;
He jumps in his cab and he's off with the pride—
Sebagoes;
He's gotta catch the boat to make Tormentine,
Then he hits up that old New Brunswick line,
Through Montreal he comes just a-flyin',
With another big load of potatoes.

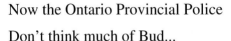

Now the Ontario Provincial Police
Don't think much of Bud...

Yeah, the cops have been lookin'
For the son of a gun
That's been rippin' the tar
Off the four-O-one;
They know the name on the truck
Shines up in the sun—"Green Gables";
But he hits Toronto and it's seven o'clock,
When he backs 'er up again
At the terminal dock,
And the boys gather 'round
Just to hear him talk
About another big load of potatoes.

Now I know a lot of people from east to west
That like the spuds from the Island best,
'Cause they'll stand up to the hardest test—
Right on the table;
So when you see that big truck a-rollin' by,
Wave your hand or kinda wink your eye,
'Cause that's Bud the Spud, from old P.E.I.,
With another big load of potatoes.

It's Bud the Spud from the bright red mud,
Rollin' down the highway smilin',
Because he's got another big load
Of the best doggone potatoes
That's ever been growed,
And they're from Prince Edward Island,
They're from Prince Edward Island.